It's a Perfect Day for a Duck

Written and Illustrated by

Paula Abare

To order additional copies of this book, contact:
Xlibris
844-714-8691
www.Xlibris.com
Orders@Xlibris.com

ISBN: Softcover   978-1-6641-5507-7
        EBook   978-1-6641-5512-1

Print information available on the last page

Rev. date: 01/28/2021

To my daughter Isis

Who is my one and only first born and to her first born,

my grandson Guglielmo,

To whom I wrote my first story for, on waiting

for his birth in The Hague, Netherlands.

It was truly a perfect day for Grandma!

IT'S A PERFECT DAY
FOR A
DUCK

IT'S A PERFECT DAY FOR A DUCK LISTENING TO THE CHICKENS IN THE BARNYARD CLUCK

IT'S A PERFECT DAY
FOR A DUCK
WATCHING THE CORN
BEING SHUCKED

IT'S A PERFECT DAY FOR A DUCK
WATCHING THEM FILL THE
BIG FEED TRUCK

IT'S A PERFECT DAY FOR A DUCK
SPLISH, SPLASHING IN
THE RAIN WITH MY
BEST FRIEND, HUCK

IT'S A PERFECT DAY FOR A DUCK
THAT I'M EATING CORN
AND NOT SOME BUGS
THAT TASTE LIKE YUCK

IT'S A PERFECT DAY FOR A DUCK
PLAYING WITH MY TURTLE
FRIENDS IN THE COOL
DARK MUCK

IT'S A PERFECT
DAY FOR A DUCK
THAT I'M NOT IN TRAFFIC
GETTING STUCK

IT'S A PERFECT DAY
FOR A DUCK
I BOUGHT THREE PINK
FLOWERS FOR A BUCK

IT'S A PERFECT DAY
FOR A DUCK
BECAUSE IT'S ALL ABOUT
LOVE AND NOT ABOUT LUCK

About the Author

Growing up in a small rural town near a lake and surrounding forest, having many encounters with wild animals, not to mention coming from a large family, there was never a lack of stories being told. Only a lack of books. To entertain myself, I learned how to draw and later added captions to those pictures.

I have traveled to many places in the world, to fairy tale weddings in Italy to the Netherlands for the birth of my three grandsons, to the tiger reserve in India, to a wonderous thousand-mile journey down the Amazon river, and to many schools in the states of America encouraging and teaching children how to read and draw.

Now as a Grandmother, living in Ashburnham Massachusetts, my three loving grandsons inspired me greatly to write those many stories that I have told around the campfire and at bedtime.